MW01034549

GLAZED HAM MURDER

THE DARLING DELI SERIES, BOOK 20

PATTI BENNING

SUMMER PRESCOTT BOOKS PUBLISHING

CHAPTER ONE

A warm spring breeze blew through the open door of Darling's DELIcious Delights. The deli was empty except for Moira Darling, her daughter Candice, and two other women. All four were wearing jeans and old shirts, and Moira had a streak of paint on her arm.

"Well, we're finished," she said, looking around at the interior of her beloved deli, which sported a fresh coat of paint. It was a touch-up that had long been needed. Moira hadn't painted the walls since she opened; the old coat had chipped and cracked in more than a few places, and was just dingy from the touch of hundreds of hands. "Thanks for helping."

. . .

"It wasn't a bad way to spend a Sunday afternoon," said Denise Donovan. The tall redhead owned the nicest restaurant in town, and was one of Moira's closest friends. It was odd to see her dressed so casually; she looked out of place without her normal sharp pantsuit and heels.

"I owe you for watching Diamond so often," said her other friend, Martha. "I was happy to help."

"We should start cleaning up," Candice said. "The pizza will be here soon, and I've got to leave in an hour to meet Eli. We're going to go visit Reggie before the movie."

"Tell me if it's good," Moira said to her daughter. "David and I might go see it later this week."

She smiled as she bent down to pick up a paint roller and a handful of brushes to rinse off at the sink in the kitchen. It felt good to have the painting finished. They hadn't even lost too much business—Sundays were the deli's shortest days anyway, and closing just two hours early had given them plenty of time to complete the project while it was still light out. She had spent the past week in a frenzy of spring cleaning both here and at home. Painting the deli had been her last project. It felt good to finally be done.

"So, what are you doing for Easter?" Martha asked, joining her at the sink with a paint tray and another roller.

"To be honest, David and I don't have any plans," Moira said. "Normally I'd want to have a nice big brunch with Candice and Eli, but they already have plans of their own, so it will probably just be the two of us."

"If you want, the two of you could come and help out with the Easter egg hunt that the library is hosting," Martha said. "I volunteered last year, and it was actually pretty fun. We'll be hiding eggs in the park, and there will be a raffle for a nice gift basket. The proceeds all go to the library."

"I'll talk to David," Moira replied.

"Oh, and they're always looking for local businesses to sponsor items for the gift basket. They like gift cards, chocolates, stuff like that."

"I can throw a gift card in," Moira said. "And I bet Candice would be happy to donate some of her candies. She's always looking for chances to get her name out there."

"Great. And let me know about helping with the Easter egg hunt, all right? We're down a couple of our usual volunteers this year."

"I will," the deli owner promised. "I'll go talk to David as soon as we're done here."

. . .

By the time the sun began to set, the deli had been cleaned up and was looking even better than it had before. The floors shone after the mopping and waxing they had received, the glass top of the counter was free of streaks and smudges, and the air still smelled slightly of fresh paint. Moira took one last, proud look at her little restaurant before she shut and locked the front door. The deli was her pride and joy; the one thing in the world—other than her wonderful daughter, of course—that she could look at and think *I made this.*

She got into her green SUV and let the engine run for a moment while she called her husband, David Morris, to see if he had made it home yet. "I'm still at the brewery," he told her. "Sorry, one of the tanks has a leak and Karissa and I have been trying to figure out where it's coming from."

"Have you had dinner yet?" she asked. "I've got some leftover pizza with me. I could stop by and drop it off before I go home to let the dogs out."

. . .

"How did I get so lucky?" he asked. She could hear the smile in his voice.

"I'll see you soon," she said with a grin of her own. She knew that *she* was the lucky one, to have found such a wonderful man to be her husband. Her first marriage had never been like this. Every day with David was so filled with happiness and caring. Sometimes it was hard to imagine how she had spent so many years without a partner like him by her side.

The microbrewery was located on a farm a few miles out of town. The property was about to go on the market for the third time in less than a year. Moira and David had discussed buying it, but neither of them really wanted to live on or manage a working farm, complete with cattle and acres of crops. Right now, David was leasing both the land and the building that the brewery used, but he owned all of the equipment. He and his sister knew that they might have to move the brewery to a different location if the next person to own the land wasn't interested in continuing the lease, but at the moment they were taking it one day at a time.

Moira parked just outside the big, boxy building that housed the office and the expensive equipment that went into making and bottling beer. She shot a glance toward the farmhouse, which had stood empty for weeks. If she believed in such things, she might almost think that this property was cursed.

She pulled her gaze away from the farmhouse and walked around to the passenger side of her vehicle to grab the pizza box. She hadn't yet admitted it to David, but part of her would be glad if the brewery had to move. This place held too many memories for her. She didn't like being reminded of her dead friend every time she walked in the door.

"Thanks for coming all the way out here," David said, greeting her with a hug and a kiss when she walked through the door.

. . .

"You're a lifesaver, Moira," said Karissa. The dark-haired woman snatched the pizza box. "I'm starved. I wasn't expecting to be here so long. David didn't tell me what was wrong when he called me in. He just said there was a problem he needed my help with. I didn't think it would mean I'd be here half the day looking over a tank full of beer."

"He's *your* brother," Moira said with a laugh. "Though you should have called me earlier. I would have been happy to bring some soup and sandwiches from the deli."

"I knew you were busy with painting; I didn't want to bother you," David said. "How did that go, by the way? Did you finish?"

"We got done a couple of hours ago and spent the rest of the time cleaning up. The deli looks like new," she told him. "Oh, before I forget, I promised Martha I'd ask you if you want to volunteer with me to help set up the Easter egg hunt in the park for the kids."

. . .

"Why not?" he said. "They've been doing that egg hunt for decades. Karissa and I used to go back when we were children. It'll be nice to help out."

"I'll tell her we'll be there, then," Moira said. "She'll be thrilled. Since Candice will be busy, I can't think of a better way to spend Easter."

CHAPTER TWO

"They're going to be here soon," Moira called up the stairs. "Are you almost ready?"

"I'll be down in a second," David called back. "Why are you so worried? Candice comes over for dinner all the time."

The anxious mother sighed. She knew that she shouldn't be so worried about the dinner. Normally she wouldn't be; as David had said, family dinners were a routine thing in the Darling-Morris household.

. . .

It was just that tonight, Candice was bringing a friend, a young woman that she had known since middle school. Candice had been an angsty teenager who once threatened to run away with Caroline Cook, her best friend. So, Moira had forbidden them from seeing each other. Shortly after that, the other girl had moved away with her parents. Now, of course, Moira and her daughter had a much better relationship, but she couldn't help but worry that the reappearance of such an old friend might bring along with it bad memories of the years just after Moira's divorce. It wasn't a time that she was eager to revisit.

She had already told all of this to David, but he just didn't understand. He was a great step-parent for Candice, but he hadn't been there during the really tough times. He had never had any children of his own, and had no way to understand the pain of watching a child grieve over a divorce.

"I'll feel better once everyone's here," Moira called back. "Which will be any minute."

· · ·

She hurried back into the kitchen to check on the food. Four perfect swordfish steaks were just about done in the oven. On the table, there was a bowl of garlic quinoa; a salad with baby spinach leaves, walnuts, and dried cranberries; a bottle of lemon-garlic vinaigrette; and a bowl of freshly made citrus pesto. Everything was perfect, and the sight of the beautifully put together meal made her relax a little. She really did love cooking.

A booming bark jolted her. Someone was here. She went back down the hall and called the two dogs back from the door. Behind her, she heard David's footsteps on the stairs. She pulled back the curtain and looked out the window next to the door to see her daughter's familiar silver convertible parked behind her SUV. Candice had already gotten out of the car, and a woman with straight black hair was standing up from the passenger seat. Next to Moira, the big, dark German shepherd gave an excited whine.

"I know, Maverick, Candice is here. She brought a friend, didn't she?"

. . .

She opened the door, letting the two dogs rush out to greet the women. Keeva, the long-legged Irish wolfhound, reached them first and greeted both of them with enthusiasm. She was so tall that her head came nearly up to their chests when she stood and looked up. Maverick took a little bit longer to warm up to the newcomer, but by the time they reached the door, he was eagerly begging for affection from both women.

"Come on in," Moira said, smiling at them. "Caroline, we can put the dogs in the other room if they're too much. I know they're pretty energetic and, well, big."

"Oh, no, I love animals," she said. "Candice has told me all about your dogs. Maverick saved your life?"

"Yes, that's a story I can tell over dinner. This is my husband, David. David, this is Candice's childhood friend, Caroline."

. . .

"It's nice to meet you," he said.

"You, too. Candice told me all about you, too. You're a private investigator? That's so cool."

He chuckled. "It really isn't as exciting as everyone seems to think it is. There's a lot of sitting around and waiting for stuff to happen, and a lot of paperwork. I do get to set my own hours though, which is nice."

"Let's go sit down," Moira said. "The fish should be done, and everything else is ready."

"I brought some salted caramel chocolates for dessert," Candice said as they walked down the hall to the kitchen. "Caroline helped me make them earlier."

. . .

"That sounds wonderful," Moira said. "It's too bad Eli couldn't make it. You said he had an important meeting?"

"Something like that," her daughter said. The smile she gave was almost mischievous. Moira raised her eyebrows, but didn't ask further. Whatever was going on, it seemed that Candice wanted to tell her in her own time.

Moira took the swordfish out of the oven and the four of them sat down around the table. David opened one of the beers from his brewery, and Moira poured the girls glasses of wine. It still felt odd to see her daughter drinking, but Candice had been of age for a while now. *It's just hard to stop thinking of her as my little girl*, she thought.

"The food is wonderful, Ms. Darling," Caroline said. "It's like something a restaurant would serve."

The deli owner smiled and thanked her. The dark-haired young woman was nothing like she had been the last time Moira had seen her. When she was younger, Caroline had been rebellious, with a penchant for breaking the rules. Now she was just as polite as Candice. Moira felt bad for trying to keep the two friends apart all those years ago, but at least it looked like they had both turned out all right.

"So, Caroline, how is North Carolina? Are you still living with your parents?"

"No, I have my own place now. It's an apartment, right on the beach."

"That sounds nice. Are you seeing anyone special?"

"Not right now," Caroline said. "I just broke up with someone, actually. I thought it would be a good time to come and visit Candice."

.   .   .

"She'll be here for a week," Moira's daughter said. "We've got a ton of stuff planned. It'll be fun."

"I bet. How's Eli doing?"

"Good." Candice made a face. "Except that his ex is in town."

"That was that Alexa girl, right?" Caroline asked. Turning to Moira, she said, "She came into the candy shop while Candice was showing me around. She kept trying to get Candice to talk about Eli. It took us forever to get her to leave."

"Eli said that he saw her at the grocery store. He's surprised that she's back. She was really upset when they broke up and she moved away."

The deli owner frowned. "It sounds like she's still interested in him."

· · ·

18

"I think she's just lonely," Candice said. "She grew up here, so she's probably just back to visit other friends. Besides, I'm not worried about it." She smiled. "I trust Eli, and I know he'll tell me if she tries anything."

CHAPTER THREE

Moira opened the fridge and frowned. She was sure that they had another ham, but she just wasn't seeing it. Easter was in a couple of days, and the glazed ham sandwiches were more popular than ever. But she couldn't make them if they didn't have the ham.

It had been two days since the family dinner with Candice and Caroline, and she was still feeling guilty about her decision to keep the friends apart years ago. It made her wonder what other mistakes she had made as a mother. She knew that she was far from perfect, but she liked to think that overall, she had been fair in raising her daughter.

. . .

She sighed with relief when she saw the ham, which had somehow been covered by packets of bacon from the butcher's recent delivery. She would have to talk with her employees about the importance of keeping things organized. To be fair, they had been more busy than usual lately. They had all been working extra to keep up with the seemingly endless stream of customers. Holidays always seemed to bring an increase in business, no matter which holiday it was.

She pulled the ham out of the fridge and unwrapped it before placing it on the cutting board. While the white bean soup simmered on the stove next to her, she cut thin slices off the ham and arranged them on a platter to make it easier for her employees to put together the sandwich that came along with the daily special.

Now that winter was over, the deli's catering service was once again in demand. They had already scheduled two weddings, a birthday party, and a corporate retreat hosted by a business from Traverse City. The last one had surprised her. She hadn't known that her little deli was famous enough to attract business from a town over an hour away. Just a couple of years ago, no one but locals had heard of Darling's DELI-cious Delights. Now people from all over Michigan seemed to know who she was.

I never wanted fame when I started all of this, she thought. *I never even thought that this little hobby of mine would bring in real money.* It still astounded her to think about how far the deli had come in such a brief time. It sometimes felt like it had spiraled out of control, though she wasn't complaining. She had managed to make a completely fresh start on her life, and she was determined to take advantage of it as best she could.

The ham sliced, Moira covered the platter with plastic wrap and put it in the refrigerator before washing her hands and pushing her way through the swinging door that led to the front room. Darrin was behind the register, and Jenny was restocking the drink fridge. The deli owner smiled. David's beer always flew off the shelves whenever he delivered a new batch. Her husband was doing very well with his new hobby. She just hoped that he and his sister managed to find a new place to set up the brewery if whoever bought the land wasn't interested in extending the lease. It really would be best if they could buy property of their own, but then they would also need to spend time putting up a suitable building and getting whatever permits they needed to run a business out of the new place.

Maple Creek had come back to life after the long winter. People were walking up and down the sidewalks carrying shopping bags and walking dogs. There were little green buds on the trees that lined Main Street, and the sky was a perfect, clear blue without a single cloud.

I hope the weather is this nice on Sunday, she thought. *I'm really going to enjoy helping out at the Easter egg hunt if it is.* She was glad that she and David were going to be volunteering their time. It would be nice to spend the afternoon with her friends, and, like David, she remembered doing the Easter egg hunt in the park when she was a child. She had taken Candice too, on the years that her daughter hadn't spent the holiday with her father.

Feeling happy, she turned to the small blackboard that listed the breakfast special and wiped it off before picking up a piece of chalk and writing the lunch special; *White bean soup and glazed ham sandwich on choice of bread.* They would continue serving the mini quiches that Darrin had made the deli so famous for until they ran out, but wouldn't be making any more until the next morning. A few customers had asked if there was any chance that they could start serving breakfast all day—their crêpes were pretty popular too—but she thought it would be too difficult to keep up with that many menu options all day long. It would mean having someone in the kitchen at all times to cook up orders, and she didn't want to have to hire a new employee unless she had to.

.   .   .

"Go ahead and start taking lunch orders," she told Darrin. "And come back and grab a bowl of soup yourself when you get a chance. You've been working all morning, you deserve a break."

"Thanks, Ms. D.," he said. "I'll grab lunch soon."

She went back into the kitchen and idly stirred the simmering soup, thinking about what she would do that weekend. The deli would close early on Saturday, and be closed all day on Easter Sunday. Even with the volunteer work she had agreed to do, she would have most of the weekend free. *If it's warm enough, maybe David and I can take the dogs to the beach*, she thought. The water would still be too chilly for humans to swim this early in the year, but the dogs didn't seem to mind. Both of them loved a good romp through the water, though brushing the sand out of their fur afterward was always a pain.

Her phone began to vibrate in her pocket. She put down the soup spoon and pulled her phone out. She always felt guilty answering it during work, since she asked her employees not to take private calls unless it was an emergency. This was a call from Candice, though, and she always made an exception for her daughter.

"Hey, sweetie," she said, leaning against the counter.

"Mom?" Her daughter's voice was tearful. Moira felt a sharp pang of fear. Her hand tightened on the phone. "I—I think my car was stolen. Can you come and help? I'm at the bar in Lake Marion."

"Your car?" Moira blinked. At least her daughter was okay. A car could always be replaced. "Of course. I'll be right there. I'm going to see if David can meet us there too, okay?"

She got off the phone and hurried out of the kitchen to tell her two employees that she had to leave. "I'm so sorry," she said. "Something came up. Will you be okay here? Can you stay a little bit later, Darrin? I know your shift is supposed to end soon."

"No problem," he said. "I hope everything is all right."

"Thanks," she said. "So do I."

CHAPTER FOUR

Moira pulled into the bar's parking lot and was relieved to see David's familiar black sedan already parked there. He was standing next to Candice, along with a pair of police officers. She shut off her SUV and hurried over.

"What happened?" she asked.

"Let Candice talk to the police," David said, taking her by the elbow and leading her a few steps away. "They need to start looking for the vehicle as soon as possible. She'll tell you once she's done, but every second the police wait the thief could be getting farther away."

"Is she okay?"

"She's fine," her husband assured her. "She's not hurt; she wasn't even here when it happened."

"Okay," Moira breathed. "Okay, that's what really matters."

It seemed to take forever for the police to finish asking her daughter questions, but at last they tucked their notebooks away and said their good-byes, promising to do everything they could to find the missing vehicle. Once they left, Moira, Candice, and David all went across the street to the diner where the private investigator bought them all lemonades.

"Thanks so much," Candice said. "Sorry, I just

completely panicked when I saw that it was gone."

"What happened?" Moira asked. "I still don't understand how it got stolen."

"Well, Caroline and I were at the bar last night and I was too buzzed to feel safe driving home, so Eli took us both home and I left the convertible in the bar's parking lot," the young woman began. She gave her mother a nervous look.

"I'm glad you did the responsible thing and got a ride home," Moira said. "Don't worry, I won't ever be mad about that. Go on."

"Well, I came back this morning to pick it up—I walked because it was nice out—and it was gone. That's it, really."

"Are you sure it didn't get towed?" her mother asked.

· · ·

"I'm sure. The bar owner said he never tows cars unless they're left there for more than a couple of days. He'd rather people park there overnight and get a taxi home, than try to drive home drunk and get in an accident."

"He's a good man," David said. "I've met him a few times. He's selling my drafts now. About your car, are you missing the keys?"

"No. There are only two copies, and Mom has the other one."

Moira dug in her purse and pulled out her key ring to make sure her daughter's spare care key wasn't missing. "Yep, I've still got it."

"And mine's right here," Candice said, holding her copy up. "I guess whoever took it must have hot-wired it.

.   .   .

"What are the police going to do?" Moira asked. "Do they think they'll be able to track down the person who took it?"

"They said they're going to put an alert out to other departments and that police all over Michigan will have their eyes peeled for it, but they can't guarantee anything. I'm supposed to bring in the title and proof of insurance as soon as I can. The officer who took my statement said I should also call the insurance company and report the vehicle stolen right away."

"We can give you a ride back to your house to get the paperwork and then to the police station," David said. "After that, I'm going to come back here and take a look around the parking lot. Do you remember which spot you parked in?"

Candice nodded. "Yeah, I remember because I parked right next to a big puddle and got my shoes all wet. I hope they find the car. I feel so bad that it got stolen." The vehicle had been a birthday gift from Moira and David the year before.

"It's not your fault, sweetie," her mother assured her. "Whoever stole it is the one I'm mad at. I guess by now I should know not to expect any better from people, but it still makes me angry to think that someone would do something like that."

"We'll find the car," David told both of them. "Right now, though, we have to follow up with the police and the insurance company."

Moira kept her eyes peeled as David drove, her heart lifting whenever she saw a silver car, only to be disappointed when she saw that it wasn't her daughter's. She knew that the thief could very well be cities —or even states—away by now, but something in her expected to see the missing car around every curve. The three of them arrived at the Maple Creek police station an hour after they left the bar, Candice still alternating between tears and anger at her stolen car.

.   .   .

Moira looked up hopefully when Detective Jefferson, the young head detective of the police force that served the two small towns, approached them, but he shook his head slightly as he met her eyes. *Still no news*, she thought. *I know it hasn't been long, but I really want them to find whoever did this.*

"You have the paperwork?" he asked Candice. She nodded. "Good. Bring it back, and we'll make photocopies. We may need the vehicle's VIN to identify it, depending on the condition it is found in."

The three of them followed the detective back to his office, a room that Moira had become familiar with over the past few years. She was glad that he was the one heading their case; she and David had both helped him in the past, and she knew that he would give her daughter's case the careful consideration that he gave every case that came across his desk.

"Right, you folks can wait here. I'll take these into

the other room and copy them. After that I'll answer any questions you may have, but there really isn't much else to do at this point other than play the waiting game. I'll send a couple of officers out to look for it when I can. It's going to be chaotic around here for a little bit, but I promise we'll keep an eye out for your car."

Candice and Moira took the chairs in front of Jefferson's desk while David stood near the door. The deli owner exchanged a glance with her husband. She knew that he would be eager to get out of there and start looking for the car on his own. He had never been able to resist a good mystery... though for that matter, neither had she.

"Mom, do you think you could—" Candice broke off mid-sentence as Detective Jefferson's office door opened to reveal a female officer who Moira didn't recognize—meaning she must have been new.

"Detective, a call just came about a— Oh, I'm so sorry. I should have knocked." She began to shut the door, then paused. "Do you know where Detective Jefferson is?"

"He was going to copy some paperwork, so wherever the copy machine is," Moira told her.

"Thanks." The young woman hurried out the door. They continued to wait for another for minutes until at last Jefferson returned. He handed the papers back to Candice and herded them out of his office.

"I'm sorry," he said. "We'll have to pick this back up later. There's been an accident with a fatality, and I'm needed at the scene."

CHAPTER FIVE

David drove the three of them back to Lake Marion so Moira could pick up her vehicle and Candice could return home where her sleepy friend was waiting to hear the story of the missing car. After dropping Candice off, Moira joined David at his office.

"So, what do you think?" she asked him. "Should I help her start car shopping?"

"Give it some time," he said. "It's a nice car, and it's bound to turn up somewhere, though I can't guess in what condition."

. . .

"Do you think someone stole it so they could sell it, or was it just some kids taking it on a joy ride?"

"Without the keys, I doubt any of our local kids would have been able to start it. That's the puzzling part. Newer vehicles are difficult to hotwire. They aren't built like they were twenty years ago. Whoever stole it must have known what they were doing."

"What would a professional car thief be doing in Lake Marion? It's a nice little town, but it's still too early in the year for there to be many tourists, and not many of the locals drive anything nice enough to be worth stealing for a profit."

Her husband grinned at her. "You know, you're quite good at asking all of the right questions. That was exactly what I was wondering myself."

. . .

"I've had plenty of practice these past few months, helping you out with cases like I have been," she said, laughing. She sobered quickly, the theft of the car still too fresh in her mind for her to feel happy for long. "What do you think, though? Was it just bad luck on Candice's part that a skilled thief happened to see her car parked in the bar's parking lot overnight?"

"It could be as simple as that," he said. "I don't like to ignore coincidences, but at this point I really don't have any other ideas. She doesn't have any enemies, does she?"

"Not that I know of." Moira frowned. "Wait, she did say something about an ex-girlfriend of Eli's being in town. Do you think that woman might have something to do with this?"

"I doubt it, but I can look into it. What was her name? Alexa?"

. . .

The deli owner nodded. "I can see if Candice knows her last name. It's probably a long shot, though."

"It's a lead," he said. "We'll follow it and see where it goes."

Moira was halfway home when her cell phone rang. She glanced at the screen, saw that it was David, whom she had just said her goodbyes to not fifteen minutes ago, and pulled over to answer the call.

"I'm glad you answered. Meet me at the police station," he told her by way of greeting. "Jefferson said he has something for us to see, and by his tone, it doesn't sound good."

"Should I get Candice?"

"No, not yet. He asked me specifically not to say anything to her yet. He didn't mention you either way, so I'm not sure he'll be happy when you show up, too, but we'll handle whatever comes up."

"All right, I'll meet you there in ten minutes," she said. Her stomach roiled with anxiety as she put the phone down and shifted the car back into drive. What on earth could have gone wrong now?

When Detective Jefferson saw her follow the private investigator into the police station, his lips tightened, but he didn't comment. She wondered why he didn't seem to want her there. If they had found the car, even if it was wrecked, what difference would her presence make?

"I'm sorry to ask this of you, David, but I thought that with your expertise, well, you might notice something I hadn't." He glanced at Moira. "Ms. Darling, do you think you could wait out here?"

He only calls me that when he's working on a case that involves me, she thought. *What's going on?*

43

.   .   .

"She's here as my assistant," David told the detective. At the other man's disbelieving look, he added, "She's been helping me out for a while now, you know that. Whatever's going on now, I'm not going to keep it from her. Consider her just another consultant."

"Fine," Jefferson said sourly. "This way, please."

They followed him to his office again. This time, he sat down in the comfortable leather chair and began typing something into the computer. She and David sat across from him. After a few seconds, he turned the screen around so it faced them.

"Earlier today, we got a call about a hit and run. The man's body was found on the side of the road by a woman walking her dogs. This video is from a surveillance camera belonging to a party store. It just barely caught the accident. I'll play the video twice, once at full speed, and once at half speed, zoomed in. The second time I play it, please observe the driver." He glanced at Moira. "The video is graphic, and I won't think any less of you if you don't want to watch it."

"I'm fine," she said shortly, her heart pounding. She was confused. What did any of this have to do with her daughter?

"Very well." With no further delay, he played the video.

Moira recognized the silver car immediately. It was Candice's. Of course, the police would need more to go on to identify the vehicle than one blurry record-ing, but she didn't have any doubts. The second time the video played, which was, as promised, zoomed in and slowed down, she kept her eyes on the driver as Detective Jefferson had instructed. What she saw made the breath whoosh out of her. It felt as if she had been punched in the gut.

· · ·

"Candice," she breathed. The quality of the video was poor enough that she couldn't make out the woman's face, but there was no mistaking that long, blonde hair streaming behind the driver in the wind. It had been a nice night, and the convertible's top had been down.

"What's the time stamp on this video?" David asked, his face unreadable.

"Just a few minutes after three in the morning," the detective said.

"The bar closed at two," the private investigator said. "That gives us an hour between the latest she would have left the bar, and when the accident happened."

"You can't actually think she did this," Moira said, looking between her husband and the police detective. "Candice wouldn't run someone over and then drive away."

· · ·

"She might if she was intoxicated," Jefferson said.

"She said she asked Eli for a ride home. Can't you confirm that with him? I know it looks like her in the video, but it could be anyone with long, light colored hair. My daughter wouldn't do something like this."

"Her fiancé isn't exactly the most reliable alibi. If anyone could be convinced to lie for her, it would be him," the detective said. "But we'll do what we can to piece this together."

"He wouldn't lie," Moira said. "I know what it looks like, but Candice did not do this."

With that, she stood up and walked out of the room, knowing that she needed space and time to process what she had seen on the video. Despite her words, she couldn't suppress the little, niggling suspicion that had taken root the instant that she had seen the driver's hair. She knew that if her daughter was in her right mind, she would never leave a hit and run victim on the side of the road. But what if last night, her daughter hadn't been in her right mind? Like Jefferson had said, too much to drink might have changed her actions.

"No," she whispered, trying now to convince herself. "Candice would never leave a man to die by himself like that. I know she wouldn't. I know it."

CHAPTER SIX

David got home late that night. Normally, Moira would have been asleep for hours, but this time she waited up for him. She had spent the evening pacing and thinking. She hated that she had to doubt her own daughter, but her eyes weren't lying. Trying to be honest with herself, she asked herself what the chances were that a car thief with long blonde hair had just happened to come across Candice's car that night. She knew that the coincidence was unlikely, but she didn't like the alternative at all.

By the time her husband walked in, she was a wreck. She gave him a quick hug, then pulled back and gazed into his face. He didn't look worried in the slightest.

"What did you find out?" she asked. He had spent the evening doing his own digging. He had suggested that she come along, but she knew that she was currently too emotional to think things through clearly, and hadn't wanted to serve as a distraction.

"Well, unless your daughter can run a mile in just over three minutes, Candice is in the clear."

Moira sat down, feeling almost dizzy with relief. "I knew she couldn't have done it. What evidence did you find?"

"Well, I talked to Eli, just casually—I didn't need him to know I was on a case—and found out that he had indeed driven Candice home last night. Shortly after they got back, her friend Caroline developed a headache. Candice gave her the last two painkillers she had, then she and Eli walked down to the convenience store on the corner to buy more and pick up a few things for breakfast before coming back and going to bed. The convenience store had a security camera, and Jefferson was able to get footage that proved that she was there when she said she was. They left the convenience store at two forty-eight in the morning, exactly."

"But I thought the accident wasn't until after three?"

"You're correct, but Jefferson and I went over the footage from the surveillance cameras in the bar's parking lot. Her car was parked out of the camera's sight, but the footage showed a woman with long blonde hair walk across the lot at two fifty-one in the morning—three minutes after Candice left the convenience store, exactly. Even if Eli had driven her back to the bar to get the car, there wouldn't have been time."

"So, it definitely wasn't her." Moira closed her eyes, too grateful and relieved to realize the implications for a few more minutes. "What happened to the car? It's still missing, isn't it?"

"It is," David said. "Considering the speed at which it hit the man the driver killed and the shards of glass and plastic on the road at the site of the accident, I'd say it has a broken headlight and dented bumper at the very least. Jefferson put a call out to local auto shops, but last I spoke to him, there hadn't been any silver convertibles in."

The matter of the missing car seemed small now that her daughter had nearly been accused of manslaughter, but she knew that they still needed to find it. "Do you know who the man that died was?" she asked her husband, realizing with a rush of guilt that she had barely even thought about the victim.

"He was a young man by the name of Joshua Russell," he said. "And I'm not sure yet if it means anything, but he was a friend of Eli's a few years back."

. . .

Moira frowned. "That does seem odd. He knew Eli, and was killed by Candice's car, driven by a woman that looked enough like her to fool even my eyes? That can't be a coincidence."

"I agree with you, but I just don't see any connection between his death and Candice and Eli, other than the car of course. We already know it couldn't have been either of them—though of course I already know neither of them would kill somebody—and according to Eli, he and Joshua hadn't spoken for years. It really might just be a coincidence and bad luck on Joshua's part."

The deli owner shook her head, too tired to think further on the subject, and too relieved to be very concerned about it. "Let's go to bed, David. I've got the afternoon shift at the deli tomorrow, but first I want to stop by Candice's and catch her up on everything. I really hope her car is found soon. Hopefully there will be evidence in it that will help the police track down the thief. I really hope whoever took the car and ran that poor man over gets the justice that she deserves."

. . .

"I hope so, too," David said. He hugged her again and brushed a kiss across her temple before releasing her. They went their separate ways; him to let the dogs out and take a shower, and her to their warm, comfortable bed to shut her eyes and relax after the long and crazy day.

CHAPTER SEVEN

When she told Candice the next morning about the hit and run and David and Jefferson's hurried detective work, her daughter was understandably upset. What Moira hadn't expected was her daughter's feeling of guilt.

"If I had just driven the car home, none of this would have happened," she said. "It's my fault that man died."

"No, it's not," the deli owner said firmly. "It's the fault of the person who hit him. You did the responsible thing and left the car at the bar after you had been drinking. I would have done the same. Don't ever second-guess a decision not to drive after you've been drinking."

"I can't believe someone used my car to murder someone," she said, still looking ill despite her mother's words.

Moira blinked. Neither she nor David had used the word murder yet. She had been considering the accident just that, an accident. But what if it wasn't? What if the mysterious thief had been targeting Joshua, and not the car. It seemed unlikely, though come to think of it, she had no idea what the young man had been doing walking down the state highway at three in the morning. Instead of looking for the car, perhaps they should be looking for the killer.

It was difficult to settle herself into her work at the deli. Her thoughts about everything that had happened the day before actually distracted her enough that she ended up burning the first batch of caramelized onions and had to scrap the entire batch and start over. Cameron poked his head into the kitchen, a concerned look on his face.

"Everything all right, Ms. D.?" he asked. "I smelled burning."

"I just wasn't paying attention," she told him. "I'll prop open the door back here to air it out." The last thing she wanted was for her customers to be turned away by the scent of burnt onions.

A few minutes later, she had another batch of chopped onion in the pan and there was a pleasant breeze blowing through the kitchen. She heard footsteps on the gravel outside and turned to see Allison walk in through the open delivery door.

"Hey, Ms. D.," she said.

"Hi, Allison. What happened to your arm?" The

young woman was wearing a sling that supported her left arm.

"Oh, I managed to strain my elbow the other day." Allison made a face. "I've got to wear this for a while to let it heal up. It sucks, but it doesn't hurt too much unless I move it."

"I'm so sorry. Will you be okay to work? I'm sure we can figure out a way to cover your shifts if we need to. I wouldn't want to ask you to do anything that will set your healing back."

"I'll be fine," she promised. "I just may ask someone else to do the chopping for a while, since it's hard to cut stuff up using only one hand."

"I think we'll be able to do that for you," Moira said with a smile. "Go on and tell Cameron that he can leave whenever he wants. I'll be out in a few minutes to write the day's special on the board."

. . .

Today she had decided to do a French onion soup with a beef and mushroom sandwich with melted Swiss cheese on toasted rye. It was one of her favorite meals. Comfort food, which she needed just then. *Maybe tomorrow I'll offer a special salad instead of a sandwich*, she thought. *If I keep making such unhealthy—if tasty—dishes, people might stop eating here so much out of concern for their waistlines.*

One pleasant thing about owning her own restaurant was that it meant that there was always a warm, tasty meal waiting for her if she got hungry. That was a double-edged sword, though, since it made it much harder for her to watch her own weight. She was all right with being a bit curvy, as long as she didn't outgrow her pants; unfortunately, her current pair were feeling a little tight.

It's hard to diet with so much else going on, she thought. *Candice's car getting stolen, the hit and run, and Easter is coming up.* She realized with a jolt that the next day was Saturday—and the day after was Easter Sunday. The holiday seemed to have snuck up out of nowhere. She still needed to go shopping for her and David's Easter breakfast, and needed to finalize things with Martha for the egg hunt. There was always so much to do.

After the soup started simmering, she switched places with Allison for a few hours, of restocking the front shelves herself to save her injured employee from having to walk back and forth carrying the heavy cases of beer, soda, meat, and cheese. Most of the products the deli carried were from local farmers, with a few exceptions such as name brand sodas and the bread from a lovely Amish family a few hours to the south. The beer, of course, was all David's brand.

The deli was not particularly busy that day. It was chilly out, and the sky was a bland grey that threatened rain. She was frowning out the window, hoping that the unpleasant weather would blow over before Sunday, when the deli's door opened and a young woman came in.

At first glance, Moira thought the woman was her

daughter. She had the same straight blonde hair, though not quite as long, and the same clear face and sharp features. She was shorter than Candice, though, and her eyes were a dark brown, not her daughter's blue. Still, the resemblance was striking, and it gave the deli owner pause.

"Welcome to Darling's DELIcious Delights," she said, realizing that she had been staring at the girl for a bit too long. "How can I help you?"

"Can I just have the special, please?" the young woman asked. "And a pop. That'll be to go."

"Coming right up." Moira ducked into the kitchen to give Allison the order, then punched the price into the register. "Will you be paying with card or cash?"

"Card," the other woman said. "Credit, if that's all right." She handed over the card. Moira glanced at it out of habit, then did a double-take when she saw the name. *Alexa.* Could this be Eli's ex, the same woman that Candice and Caroline had spoken about during dinner earlier in the week?

She ran the card through the machine and handed it back to the woman, tempted to ask, but not sure she could think of a way to do so that wouldn't make her seem like a crazy person. Reluctantly, she handed Alexa the bag of food and told her to have a good day.

Did they say she was blonde? she thought. *Or did they not mention her hair color?* She had thought Allison and Candice looked alike, but it was uncanny how similar Candice and Alexa were. After staring at the door for a few moments, the deli owner shook herself and got back to work. She had enough on her plate right now without wondering about something that was probably nothing more than a coincidence.

CHAPTER EIGHT

Easter morning dawned clear and warm. Moira left David asleep in bed and went downstairs, followed closely by two energetic, and hungry, dogs. She let them out the back door, then turned on the coffee machine and sat down at the kitchen table to wait for her required morning dose of caffeine. The birds outside were singing, and she smiled at the sound. She still felt a pang whenever she thought of the house that she had lived in for twenty years—the house that Candice had grown up in—which had burnt down the year before, but overall, she was happy here. She loved the privacy of her property, and the peace that living outside of town brought. It was as if her and David's little stone house was a world apart from the small but sometimes busy town of Maple Creek.

The coffee maker gurgled then went silent. She rose, poured her cup, and stepped out back to enjoy the first few sips in the fresh morning air with the dogs. It was a pity that they couldn't come to the Easter egg hunt later that afternoon, but she knew that she would be far too busy to keep an eye on them. Though she knew that they had no inkling of the holiday, she was determined to do something special for the two pooches who filled so much of her heart and her time.

It was a nice morning for mid-April, but still a bit chilly, and she had goosebumps on her arm by the time she went back inside with the dogs and a half-empty cup of coffee. To her surprise, her husband was up and standing in the kitchen, with what looked like half of the fridge's contents on the counter top.

"Good morning," she said. "I thought you'd still be

in bed for a while yet. I was going to make breakfast for us both in a little bit."

"No need," he said with a smile. "I thought I would make us omelets."

She raised an eyebrow, touched and surprised. Although David could cook, he usually preferred to buy his food already made and ready to eat whenever possible.

"That sounds nice," she said. "An omelet would hit the spot. Would you mind setting a couple of the eggs aside for the dogs? I was going to scramble some up for them as a special treat for their breakfast."

The omelet that David made really did hit the spot. It was beautifully spiced, chock full of vegetables and cheese, and cooked to perfection in a well-buttered pan. It wasn't quite the healthy meal that Moira had been planning but it was definitely worth it. Besides, everyone knew that any food consumed on holidays was empty of calories. She could start her diet tomorrow.

"Happy Easter, David," she said, pausing by his chair to give him a kiss as she cleared her place. "And thank you for agreeing to help out at the egg hunt today. It will be nice to spend the holiday together."

"It's a day for family," he agreed. "Work can wait."

Neither of them mentioned the case of the missing car and the dead man. Somehow Easter Sunday didn't seem like the time to talk about such dark things. Moira still kept a close eye on her phone, hopeful for news about the search for the vehicle, but after so many days, she was no longer constantly on edge about it. She knew that Detective Jefferson still seemed to have hopes that it would turn up, but she had already turned her mind to practical solutions for getting her daughter another car.

. . .

After a leisurely morning together at the house, Moira and David got into her SUV and drove the short distance into town. The Easter egg hunt was supposed to start in two hours, and the half of the park that the library was using was roped off with polite signs asking people to stay off the grass until the hunt began. The other half of the park was already filled with people enjoying the nice weather. The deli owner smiled, the sight reminding her of all of the cookouts and birthday parties she and Candice had had there over the years.

"Moira! Over here."

She looked toward the empty half of the park to see her friend, Martha, waving at her. A small group, mostly women, were gathered around a picnic table, laughing and chatting while they unloaded a minivan packed with supplies. Moira grabbed David by the arm and led him over to the group.

"I'm glad you could make it," Martha said, giving her a quick hug. "The deli's not open today?"

. . .

"We're closed for Easter," Moira said. "It's nice for the employees to be able to spend the day with their families. I always feel bad for the people who have to work on holidays."

"Me, too. Though come to think of it this is the first Easter in a couple of years that I haven't been busy trying to fit work in around helping out with this. Sometimes I wish I had a job where I didn't take my work home with me."

"Well, you're always welcome to come and work at the deli," she told her friend, grinning. "The pay isn't great compared to what you make now, and the morning shift starts at six-thirty, but when you walk out the door, you're done." *Well, unless you're me*, she thought.

"Maybe I'll take you up on that in another ten years," Martha said with a laugh. "It sounds tempting, but I know I would go stir-crazy after a few weeks."

. . .

It was nice, spending time with Denise and Martha and the other women. David and a couple of the other men volunteered to hide the plastic eggs once the women had filled them with candy, so Moira spent most of her time counting out jelly beans and chocolate kisses.

"Don't forget not to hide any by the river," Martha called as the first set of eggs was taken away. "We wouldn't want anyone falling in. And don't forget that you're hiding these for little kids. What's eye level for you will be way over their heads."

"How many eggs are there?" Moira asked as she began filling yet another plastic egg with candy. "And what happens if the kids don't find them all?"

"There are exactly two hundred," Martha told her. "I counted them twice this morning. The child who finds the most gets a gift certificate to the library's monthly book sale. Not many kids care too much about the prize, but they like the idea of winning, so it keeps them from stealing the eggs. We count them all, and if more than a couple are still missing by the end of the day we'll go and look for them. And then ask the guys to hide them in easier spots next time. The kids normally do a pretty good job of finding them, though."

"I remember how much Candice used to love this." She looked down at the little plastic egg in her hands, and realized it had been years since she had hidden a real egg for eager little hands to find. Would she ever have the chance to host an Easter egg hunt at her own house for her family again? Maybe she would have grandchildren one day. The thought made her smile, though she still felt too young in her late forties for anyone to start calling her Grandma.

"How is she doing?" Martha asked, tossing yet another egg into a basket. "I heard about her car."

"She's pretty upset, as you can imagine. At least it

isn't much of an interference, since she can walk most places she needs to go, and Eli is always happy to give her a ride."

"Tell her I'm sure the car will turn up eventually. Did I ever tell you I had my car stolen a couple of years ago? I was in Grand Rapids, and I left it running in the parking lot while I ran into a store to pick something up, and when I came out, it was gone. It was found a few blocks away in a parking lot, perfectly fine. I needed to buy a new set of keys, though. That was a pain."

The deli owner realized her friend didn't know about the hit and run. She didn't want to bring the subject up now, but she doubted that her daughter's car would be found in any sort of good condition. And when it *was* found, if it ever was, there was no telling how long it would take the police to finish gathering all of the evidence from it. One way or another, she knew her daughter would have to wait quite a while to get behind the wheel of her pretty silver convertible again.

CHAPTER NINE

The Easter egg hunt started at two in the afternoon, but people kept trailing in until almost three. Two hundred eggs had seemed like quite a lot to Moira when Martha told her the number, but seeing how many young children were there to look for them, she wondered if there were enough.

Even with all of the eggs hidden, the volunteers weren't off the hook. They had to walk around the park, supervising the egg hunt and making sure that none of the children wandered into the off-limits areas: down by the river, on the bridge, or near the roads. Moira and David walked along the path near the trees by the river, keeping an eye out for straying children.

She was watching a pair of girls who looked to be around eight as they searched in the bushes near the trees when one of them tripped over something and fell to her knees. She hurried over to help the girl up.

"Look at your tights, Ella, they're all muddy," the other girl said. The one who fell looked down and immediately started crying. Wincing, the deli owner tried to comfort her.

"I'm sure they can be washed. The important thing is that you aren't hurt. No scrapes or bruises?"

The girl shook her head. "No, but I dropped my basket."

"Yeah, I saw. Your eggs all rolled down the hill," the

other girl said, grinning. The girls must have been sisters, Moira thought, because only a sister would find that funny. "I'm gonna win and I'm gonna go tell Mom you wrecked your tights."

"That's not fair, I had more eggs than you," the first girl whined.

"Well we aren't allowed to go down by the river, and plus Mom said we had to stay where she could see us."

"Give me some of your eggs, then,"

"No way, it's not my fault that you fell."

David spoke, cutting short what seemed about to become an all-out fight between the two girls. "Look, I'll go see if I can find the eggs that rolled down the hill. Ms. Darling can take you back to your mom so you can get cleaned up, and I'll meet you all over at the tables, okay?"

This got nods all around. Moira led the two girls back toward the adults near the entrance of the park, pausing every so often so one of the girls could dash off to check a clump of grass for eggs. She was glad that David had volunteered to go into the trees and down the muddy hill to look for the missing eggs— she was wearing heels and a brightly colored dress of her own, and would probably have come back up the hill just as muddy as the girl beside her was.

It only took a few minutes for David to find them. He returned the lost eggs to the girl, accepted thanks from her mother, and then pulled Moira to the side. She looked up at him and was about to ask him how it had gone when he spoke.

"We need to call the police," he said. "I found Candice's car down by the river."

· · ·

Detective Jefferson met them down by the river fifteen minutes later. He was wearing a suit. Moira realized that they must have called him away from his own Easter celebrations. She felt bad to think that they must have interrupted a church service, or maybe a family dinner.

"Well, that's it," he said. He seemed surprised, as if he hadn't actually expected to see the silver car there. "I'm surprised no one stumbled onto it before today."

The car wasn't well hidden. It was just parked there, next to the river, with its top down. The right head-light was broken, and there was a smear of some-thing dark on the grill that she didn't want to look too closely at. Her daughter's car, a murder weapon. The thought gave her shivers.

"It doesn't look like whoever stole it wanted to hide it," David agreed.

.   .   .

"It could have been moved, I suppose," Jefferson mused.

"Well, it must have been here since Friday, at least," Moira said. Both men looked at her in surprise. "Well, the last time it rained was Friday, and the interior is wet. No one would have been driving it like that. So it must have been sitting out here for that long, at least."

"That's observant of you," Jefferson said. "I think you're right."

"People may have seen it, but didn't think to report it," David said. "People do come down to the river to fish, but the fishing is better upstream a bit where there are fewer sticks and weeds in the water. There probably weren't too many pedestrians down here in the past week."

"What now?" the deli owner asked.

. . .

"We'll get it towed to the police lot, and begin going over it," Jefferson said. "Since it was used in a crime, it may be a while before your daughter gets it back. At least you'll be able to tell her that we know where it is and it's mostly in one piece, though I'm not sure how difficult it will be to fix the water damage. Have you touched anything?"

"No," David told him. "I walked around it to look for damage, but did not touch the vehicle."

"Good." The police detective approached the car and peered inside. His lips pulled down in a frown. "Open alcohol containers," he muttered. "Does your daughter drink beer, Ms. Darling?"

"Maybe once in a while," Moira said. "She's of age, so I don't see why it should matter. We already know she wasn't driving the car during the hit and run incident. And she left the car at the bar after having a couple of drinks, for goodness' sake. She's not going to drink and drive."

· · ·

He nodded slowly, continuing his walk around the vehicle. At last he looked up. "You two are free to leave. I'll get a tow truck down here and my men will begin trying to figure out what happened here. I'm sure your daughter will be glad to hear that her car has been found."

Moira and David left the detective to his work. The deli owner wasn't quite sure how she was feeling. Why had he asked that question about Candice? Didn't the video footage prove that the woman who had stolen the vehicle couldn't have been her daughter? Was it possible that Detective Jefferson still suspected that Candice had something to do with that hit and run?

CHAPTER TEN

Moira dropped David off at their house before driving out to Lake Marion to talk to her daughter. She knew that the car having been found should be good news, but somehow, she couldn't shake the bad feeling she had about the way Detective Jefferson had questioned her about her daughter. Why did she feel like their lives had just gotten so much more complicated?

Her phone buzzed and she glanced at it. Her daughter was at the candy shop, though Moira was sure the young woman had told her that Candice's Candies would be closed for the day. *Maybe she decided to open up for a few hours*, she thought. *I'm sure a candy shop would be a popular destination on Easter.*

When she got there, the shop was dark. Confused, she drove around back. The parking lot was empty, but since her daughter didn't have a car at the moment, that was to be expected. She parked a few spots away from the rear entrance and knocked on the door. A second later, Candice opened it. She had a smudge of what looked like pink icing on her face.

"Hey, Mom. Happy Easter. Come on in."

"Happy Easter, sweetie. What are you doing?" the deli owner asked, looking around the kitchen in curiosity. Ingredients were strewn about, and Caroline was carefully watching something that was bubbling away on the stove.

"Caroline wanted to learn how to make some of the candy I sell," Candice said. "We're doing some Easter chocolates right now. They should still sell pretty well next week—that is if we don't eat them all first."

"I'm sure that between Eli and the two of you, it'll be close," Moira said. "Where is he, anyway?"

"Oh, he's taking Reggie out to eat. We went to church together this morning, and he'll be back in time for the movie tonight."

"I'm surprised you're not eating with them. I know Reggie just adores you."

"Eli's supposed to be talking to him about something," Candice said. The mischievous look was back in her eyes. "I thought I should let them have some privacy."

"Hi, Ms. Darling," Caroline called, looking up from the stove. "Candice, the thermometer is at the right temperature. What should I do?"

. . .

"Turn off the burner and begin pouring the chocolate into the molds," Candice said. "Do you need help this time?"

"I think I've got it," the other woman said.

While the Caroline began preparing the silicone molds, Candice pulled open the fridge and offered her mother a drink. "We've got some lemonade, water, of course, milk—though I mostly use that for cooking—and I guess that's it. I need to stock up again, I guess. It gets so warm in here. Logan and I go through a lot of cold drinks."

"I'll have some of that lemonade," Moira said. "It looks great. Thanks."

She took the bottle and leaned against the counter, watching as Caroline carefully filled each mold to just below the rim. She had always been impressed by the beautiful candies her daughter made. She was glad to see that her friend was taking an interest in it, too.

"I've got good news," she said to Candice. "We found your car."

"Really? Mom, that's great! Why didn't you say something sooner? Where was it?"

"It was down by the river in the park in Maple Creek," she said. "It looked like it had been there for a while. The top was left open, and there's some water damage inside."

The young woman's face fell, then brightened again. "Well, I guess it's better than it could have been. I was afraid I was never going to see it again."

"You know, before you can get it back, the police are

going to have to go over it for evidence regarding the man's death. It might take a while."

"I know. I hope they find out who took it. Eli can keep giving me rides until they're done with it."

"I'm all done with these molds," Caroline said. "I'm going to put them in the fridge, then I'll go up front and make space in one of the display cases for the chocolate."

"Thanks," Candice said. "I'll join you in a second, but I want to hear more about my car first."

Moira obliged, describing the condition of the vehicle as best as she could. She skipped over the part about the blood on the grill, feeling the urge to protect her daughter from the more gruesome details even after all these years.

"Detective Jefferson said he found some open

containers of alcohol in it," she said. "I noticed some empty bottles of David's beer when I walked by it on my way back up the hill." She fell silent, not wanting her daughter to think that she was accusing her of anything, but also needing to hear from the young woman herself that she hadn't been the one drinking those beers in the car.

"Weird," Candice said. She picked up the empty pan of melted chocolate and took it to the sink to rinse it out.

"Candice, it looked like someone had been drinking them while they were driving."

"Maybe that's why the person who stole my car hit that poor guy," her daughter said. "It makes me so mad. I left my car at the bar so I wouldn't chance accidentally hurting someone, and then someone else steals it and kills someone with it! It's just not right." She put the pan down in the sink hard enough that the clang made Moira's ears ring. Still, she relaxed. Her daughter hadn't been drinking in the car. It had been foolish of her to even suspect her for a moment. When would she learn to trust the people that she loved the most?

"I'm sorry, sweetie," she said. "Just remember, it wasn't your fault."

The door to the kitchen opened and Caroline poked her head through. "Sorry to interrupt, but Candice, that girl is back. You've got to come and see this."

Candice traded a glance with her mother. The two women followed Caroline into the front room, where Moira saw a blonde girl that she recognized. It was the woman named Alexa, the one that she had thought might be the ex of Eli's that her daughter and her friends had spoken of.

"Sorry," Caroline whispered. "She knocked on the door and I didn't recognize her until I had already opened it. It felt too rude to ask her to leave by then."

.   .   .

Candice frowned but approached the woman anyway. "Hey, Alexa. What're you doing here? We're closed today."

"Sorry, I just saw someone through the window and thought you might have just forgotten to flip the sign over. By the way, you have something pink on your face."

Candice wiped at the smear of pink frosting in irritation. "Did you want something? Even though we aren't open, I guess I could boot up the register."

"No, I just wanted to say hi." The woman gave a bright smile. "You know, I expected to hate Eli's new girlfriend, but you seem so nice."

"Fiancée," Candice said. "I see you changed your hair."

"Yeah." Alexa ran her fingers through her light

blonde hair. "I thought a change from my boring brown might be nice."

Caroline made an odd sound. Moira glanced over to see that she was trying to keep from laughing.

"Well, thanks for stopping by," Candice said with icy politeness. "Maybe I'll see you some other time." Moira admired the skill with which Candice herded the other woman out the door, knowing she wouldn't have been as graceful. Candice locked the door, turned around, and gave an exaggerated sigh.

"What was all of that about?" Moira asked, looking between her daughter and her daughter's friend.

"That girl is still obsessed with Eli," Caroline said, grinning. "It's so weird. I'm pretty sure she got her hair bleached to look more like Candice. What's next, blue contacts? It's like she thinks if she looks more like Candice, Eli will take her back. Of course, we all know he's crazy in love with this girl right here." She put an arm around Candice's shoulders.

"I really do hope she doesn't plan on being in town for long," the other girl said. "I trust Eli, but I still don't like the thought of his ex hanging around all the time."

The deli owner trailed after the other two women as they headed back toward the kitchen. She was deep in thought. A woman who looked strikingly like her daughter, with dyed blonde hair, and a grudge against Candice... was it possible that Alexa had stolen the car?

CHAPTER ELEVEN

Moira woke up with a headache the next morning. She rolled out of bed with a groan, and muttered darkly when she looked outside the bedroom window. The rain was pelting down so hard that she couldn't even see the trees across the yard. Wind gusted, and the droplets fell sideways for a few moments. She glanced at her alarm clock, and was surprised to see the numbers still glowing solidly at her. It was surprising that they hadn't yet lost power.

She pulled on her bathrobe and went downstairs to find David already up and in the kitchen, sipping coffee and staring out the window. He looked around when he heard her come into the room.

. . .

"Good morning," he said. "Did I wake you?"

"No." She covered her mouth as she yawned. "I think the storm did. Why are you up so early?"

"Maverick had to go out, and I guess he decided it was my turn to do it," David said. "That cold nose on him is quite the weapon when he wants it to be."

She heard a whine and turned to see the German shepherd locked behind the gate that blocked off the mudroom. He was soaking wet. Keeva, on the other hand, was lying on the kitchen rug, her fur dry as a bone.

"She didn't want to go out?"

"She refused to so much as set a paw out the door,"

he said. He looked out the window again. "I can't say I blame her."

"At least yesterday was nice," Moira said as she poured herself a cup of coffee. "It's been such a wet spring. I hope it doesn't rain this much all summer."

"I'm sure it will calm down as the weeks go by," he said. "Are you still going to open the deli this morning?"

"I should," she said reluctantly. "People are still going to stop by on their way to work and to school, and I would hate for them to go out of their way just to find that the deli is closed."

He nodded. "Just drive safely. I probably won't go anywhere until it calms down. Thank goodness I don't have to follow anyone around today."

She sat down across from him at the kitchen table.

PATTI BENNING

"Nothing from Jefferson yet, I take it?"

"Not yet. It's a shame that the car wasn't found before the rain on Friday. I'm sure some evidence was destroyed. It would have been even worse after this, though." He gestured toward the window.

"At least she seems to be taking it well," Moira said. "Any luck on digging anything up about Alexa?"

"Nope. She's never had so much as a speeding ticket. I don't know how or where she would have learned to steal a car. I gave Jefferson her name anyway, just in case he can find a link. They found some blonde hairs on the driver's seat, which are being analyzed in a lab. Of course, chances are they're Candice's, but the examination will show whether any of the hairs have been bleached. Does Candice get highlights?"

"She hasn't recently," Moira said. "She's done it in the past, but didn't like how it turned out."

· · ·

96

"Well, then if any of the hairs have been bleached, Jefferson might have a reason to take a closer look at Alexa."

"It scares me to think that someone might be out there that wishes my daughter harm," Moira said. "I don't like this ex of Eli's at all." She fell silent and sipped her coffee, thinking all the while. "Do you think Alexa would have had any reason to kill Joshua? I know he was a friend of Eli's a while back. Is it possible that they knew each other?"

"It's possible," he said. "That's something you should ask Candice. Or Eli himself."

"That reminds me, I think the two of them and Reggie are up to something," she said. She told him about the mysterious meetings that Eli had been having, and they spent the rest of the time until she had to leave for work tossing ideas back and forth about what her daughter was plotting.

· · ·

Despite the umbrella that she unfurled the second she stepped out of the car, Moira was soaking wet by the time she'd unlocked the deli's door and let herself inside. At least it was warm and dry inside the building.

She stripped off her damp coat and hung it in the kitchen where the heat of the stove would dry it. Her umbrella she shook off and left by the back door. She flicked the coffee maker on and pulled out a carton of eggs to begin preparing the morning's mini quiches. She was feeling jittery from drinking so much coffee on an empty stomach, and decided that the first quiche that came out of the oven would be hers.

The sound of the storm blowing outside the building combined with the comforting sounds and scents of a kitchen made her feel oddly secure and comfortable that morning as she worked. There was just something about the sound of rain on a roof that always made her happy.

. . .

It wasn't until after she finished her breakfast of a garlic and artichoke quiche and a blueberry crêpe topped with powdered sugar that she remembered her promise to start her diet today. *Well, I'll start dieting at lunch,* she thought. *One meal isn't going to set me back that much.* Doing her best not to feel guilty, she rinsed off her plate and washed her hands before arranging the remaining mini quiches on a platter to put under the warming light in the special display case out front. The crêpes she made to order, so she simply covered the bowl of batter with plastic wrap and put it back in the fridge until she needed it.

She looked around the clean kitchen, glanced at the timer on the stove which was counting down the time remaining until the next batch of quiches came out, and then looked at the clock on the wall. The morning chores were done, and she still had a few minutes before it was time to open. She was getting good at this.

Figuring that she might as well take advantage of

her extra time, she sat down with her phone and sent a text message to Candice.

I need to ask Eli something. Will he be at the ice cream shop this afternoon?

She wasn't expecting a reply right away—she knew her daughter enjoyed sleeping late—so she was surprised when her phone buzzed just a few seconds later.

We're going out to brunch today in Maple Creek. We can stop at the deli after.

She texted back, *Perfect.* She wondered if this line of investigating would go anywhere, or lead to yet another dead end. It was worth a try, at least. Something about Alexa made her uncomfortable. The thought that the woman was trying to emulate her daughter frightened her. At least Candice seemed to be handling the girl's intrusions well enough, for now at least.

CHAPTER TWELVE

Since her daughter had mentioned brunch, Moira wasn't expecting to see them until after eleven at the earliest. She was surprised when Caroline walked through the door shortly after ten, looking as wet and bedraggled as everyone else had that morning. The power had already dimmed twice, and the deli owner had spent the last ten minutes trying to remember whether she had unplugged the computer at home in case of a power surge; she hoped it hadn't completely slipped her mind. She had a suspicion that it had.

"Hi, Caroline," she said. She peered around the

dark-haired young woman, looking for her daughter. "Is Candice with you?"

"No," her daughter's friend said. "She and Eli are meeting someone. I didn't feel like I should be there, so I offered to wait here. I hope that's all right."

"Of course, that's fine. What are they doing?"

Caroline smiled. "I think Candice wants to tell you herself."

Moira knew that she should just be patient, but she was dying to know what it was that Candice and her fiancé had up their sleeves. If they decided to forego their beautiful destination wedding and elope, she was going to be upset. Of course it was Candice's choice, but she had always dreamed that her daughter would have a perfect traditional wedding, surrounded by friends and family. Moira was looking forward to her part in the ceremony, and was also excited for the chance to travel somewhere nice with David. It had only been a few months since her own honeymoon, but she already missed the excitement of vacation.

"Do you want something to eat while you wait?" Moira asked as the young woman took a table. "It's on the house. We're still serving breakfast, but I could whip you up a sandwich if you'd prefer."

"Actually, breakfast sounds great." She eyed the blackboard for a moment. "How about some crêpes?"

"Sure. What filling?"

"Raspberries?" Caroline asked.

"Coming right up," Moira said with a smile. "Help yourself to a drink. Or do you want coffee?"

. . .

"Pop's fine. Thanks, Ms. Darling."

The deli owner returned a few minutes later with a pair of freshly made crêpes. She set the plate down, then said, "Is it all right if I sit with you, Caroline? It's been pretty slow so far this morning, and I'd feel odd just sitting at the register while you're over here all by yourself."

"Sure, the company will be nice. But I'm not going to tell you what Candice and Eli are doing."

Moira laughed. "Don't worry, I won't try to get you to say anything about that. Even though it's driving me crazy, I respect her enough to wait until she's ready to tell me in her own time."

She sat and glanced outside while the other woman began eating. Was it all in her mind, or did the rain look like it was slowing down a little? If it cleared up, she might actually start getting some customers in.

· · ·

"So," she said, turning back to Caroline. "How do you like being back in Michigan?"

"It's nice," she said. "I'm thinking of moving here, actually. Candice said she could use someone else to help out at the candy shop, and there are a few places up for rent in town I might look at."

"What about your schooling?" Moira asked. "And your parents? I'm sure they'd miss you."

The young woman shrugged. "Maybe it's time for me to do my own thing. Besides, Candice only has an Associate's Degree, and look how well she's doing. I'm sure I could figure things out as well."

"Just make sure you have a backup plan," the older woman said. "In Candice's situation, I was behind her every step of the way. If something went wrong or the store just wasn't successful, she could always have moved back in with me. I just don't want to worry about you being here all alone, with no family to watch out for you."

"It's nice of you to care, but you shouldn't worry. I'll be fine."

"Well, all right." Moira decided to change the subject. "Have you and Candice spoken at all about her car? Who do you think could have stolen it?"

"I don't know." The dark-haired woman frowned.

"What is it?"

"It's just... no, never mind."

"You can tell me. Do you think you might know who it was? Whoever did it is responsible for a man's death, you know."

·　·　·

"I know." Caroline looked pale. "That's why I don't want to say."

It was Moira's turn to frown. "Caroline, what is it?"

"It's just that when I got up to use the bathroom that night, I noticed that Candice wasn't there. Her keys and purse were gone. I thought then that she must have just gone back for her car—she didn't like leaving it behind—and went back to bed. Then in the morning when I heard what had happened, I was so surprised. I know it's terrible of me, but I can't help but think... what if she went back to get the car, and then had the accident?"

Caroline's words sent ice through Moira's veins. She'd thought the exact same thing, though she would never admit it to anyone other than her husband. She didn't know how to respond to the young girl. It took her a long time to come up with something to say.

. . .

"Caroline," she said at last, "you know Candice. She's a good girl. Even if she did make a mistake, she wouldn't lie about it. And besides, we have proof that the driver of the vehicle wasn't her."

"Proof?"

"Yes," Moira said firmly. "I don't know if I should tell you what it is, since the police are still investigating, but I can promise you that Candice had nothing to do with that poor man's death."

After that, Caroline finished her meal in silence while Moira thought about her daughter. She hoped that this investigation was over soon, for all their sakes. If Candice's own friend thought she might be hiding something, then what would the general public think? She felt a rush of anger toward the person responsible for all of this. They wouldn't get away with this, not if she and David had a say.

When Candice finally walked in a little bit later,

Moira was in a testy mood. The sight of the wide smile on her daughter's face served to make her feel better, but just a little bit.

"Good news?" she said.

"Great news," Candice replied.

"Do I get to hear what it is?"

"Not yet, but soon," her daughter promised. "I'll tell you tomorrow, actually. Do you think you and David have time tomorrow evening for dinner to say goodbye to Caroline before she leaves, and so Eli and I can share our news with both of you at the same time?"

"I'm sure we'll be able to make it work," Moira said. "Where do you want to have dinner?"

`   .   .   .

"I was wondering if it would be all right if we could all meet at the brewery, and go from there? Caroline hasn't had a chance to see it yet."

"I'll talk to David, but that should be fine."

"Hey, Ms. D.," Eli said. "Candice said you wanted to ask me something?"

"Oh, right. I have a question about your friend that got killed, Joshua."

"Sorry to disappoint you, but I haven't been his friend for a couple of years," Eli said.

"I think you can help me anyway. Was there any chance that he knew your ex, Alexa?" Seeing his look of confusion, she went on, "Is there any reason that you can think of that she would have had to kill him?"

. . .

To her surprise, the normally mild-mannered Eli clenched his jaw, and his eyes showed a flash of anger. "Oh, she knew him, all right."

Candice stepped in. "She cheated on Eli with Joshua. That's why they broke up, and why he and Josh stopped being friends. Why are you asking all of this, Mom?"

Moira took a deep breath. "Because I think Alexa might have stolen your car and killed Joshua, and I think she was trying to frame you when she did it."

CHAPTER THIRTEEN

She checked her phone for what felt like the hundredth time that day. Still nothing. When would Jefferson make the arrest? She couldn't stand this waiting.

"Just relax, Moira," David said, reaching over to put a hand on her knee, not taking his eyes from the road. "Stressing yourself out won't make the police work any faster. Let's enjoy our evening with Candice and Eli, all right? There's no point in worrying about something you can't change."

. . .

"You make it sound so easy," she sighed, but his words did make her feel a bit better. She felt as if she had been sitting on the edge of her seat ever since she, David, and Candice had shared everything they knew about Eli's ex-girlfriend with the police yesterday afternoon. She just wished they had gone to the authorities sooner. No one seemed to know where Alexa was, and the police had spent the better part of the morning searching for her.

"We can go out to celebrate when they catch her," he said. "The Redwood Grill. I'll treat the four of us. How does that sound?"

"Like it would be terrible for my diet." She smiled. "It sounds wonderful."

He laughed and squeezed her leg before putting his hand back on the wheel so he could turn into the driveway that led to the microbrewery. The for-sale sign now read *Sale Pending*.

· · ·

"Great," he muttered. "It looks like I'll be meeting the new owners soon."

"Even if they do decide to terminate the lease, I'm sure you and Karissa will find somewhere else for the brewery," she said. "If worse comes to worst, we can buy a small plot of land near town and set something up there. It might take some time, but we'll come up with a solution."

"Thanks," he said. "I really appreciate how supportive you've been with all of this. I know it's probably not what you wanted, me being so busy all the time, so I really mean it when I say thanks."

"I just want you, well, both of us, to be happy," she said. "Watching you with the brewery, that makes me happy. You still come home to me every night, so I'm not complaining. Plus, sometimes I work some crazy hours, too."

. . .

"We're the perfect match." He gave her one last smile before he pulled into his usual spot in front of the building that housed the brewery and shut off the engine. "Time to go give Caroline that tour."

The tour didn't take long. Caroline seemed interested in everything that went into making beer, and asked David plenty of questions. Candice and Eli, on the other hand, seemed distracted. Moira watched the exchange, feeling like she was about to burst with curiosity. What on earth could they have planned?

"That's super neat," Caroline said as they left the building. "I've never been in a brewery before. The tanks are so big."

"This is just a small setup," David told her. "In an industrial-scale brewery, everything is much larger."

"Do you think your brewery will ever get that big?"

· · ·

He chuckled. "I don't plan on it. This is just a hobby. It makes enough money to pay for itself, but that's about it. I don't want or need to spend all of my time growing this business. If Karissa—that's my partner, and also my sister—ever decides that she wants to start selling our drafts on a larger scale, I'll support her, but I'm happy with how things are now."

Moira slipped her arm through David's as they left the building. The sun had just started its final descent, and the sky was beginning to change colors. It was a wonderful evening, though the ground was still wet from the rainstorm the day before.

"Well, where to now?" she asked her daughter as David paused to lock up behind them. "Where did you want to eat?"

"Just follow us," Candice said. She walked toward her car, then, to Moira's surprise, past it. Pausing mid-stride, she turned to look at her mother. "Coming?"

. . .

Moira and David traded a glance. The deli owner shrugged in response to his wordless question. She didn't have the faintest idea what her daughter was doing, but it seemed like for now they ought to go along with it. They followed the younger couple toward the empty farmhouse, with Caroline trailing along behind them on her phone. Candice walked up the porch, then paused at the door.

"You ready?" she asked Eli. He nodded. She reached into her pocket, took out a key, and inserted it into the lock. Turning to look at her mother, she smiled. "Eli and I want to welcome you to our new home."

It took Moira a moment to process those words. She stared at her daughter, then up at the imposing house. Looking back down at her daughter, she said, "You bought this place?"

Candice nodded, beaming. "We closed yesterday. That's who we went out to brunch with."

.   .   .

"I don't understand. How? Why?"

"Come on in," her daughter said. "I'll tell you inside."

The interior of the farmhouse was similar to how Moira remembered it. The biggest difference she saw was the large card table in the center of the room with chips, dip, and various drinks on top of it.

"There are hot dogs in the kitchen," the young woman said. "And we've got ice cream in the freezer. We haven't really had a chance to move anything over yet."

"I'm still in shock," Moira said. "How did you afford this place?"

"Well, since it's been on the market twice in the past year, and for such dark reasons both times, it actually didn't cost that much. And, you know, the candy shop is doing pretty well, and Eli's ice cream shop has been doing okay. It really wasn't that hard to qualify for the loan."

"Why would you *want* to buy this place?" She knew that she probably wasn't reacting to the news as well as her daughter had expected her to, but she was too shocked to try to pretend to feel anything other than what she really did, which was surprise and confusion.

"There were quite a few reasons that went into our decision," she said. "First of all, we just like the location. It's right in between the two towns, and we both like the idea of living out in the country. It's bigger than Reggie's old house in town, and there's a lot more room for things like a garden, or maybe even a swimming pool one day. Since there are bedrooms on the ground floor, Reggie will be able to come here and live with us, instead of at his nursing home. It will cost about the same to hire a nurse to come out here, but here, he'll be with family."

· · ·

"Is that what Eli was meeting with him about last week?"

"Yeah," Candice said. "He was concerned that he would get in our way, but Eli convinced him that we both wanted him to be here with us."

"Sweetie, what in the world are you going to do with a farm?"

"We're going to rent out the fields to the neighboring farmers, which will also help bring in more money, and the person who keeps his cows here has employees that stop by every day to milk them and take care of them. He's going to pay us in milk, which Eli is going to use to make the ice cream for his shop—yet another thing that should bring in more money. And, of course, David can keep the brewery here as long as he wants. Plus, we'll have plenty of room when we want to start a family a few years down the road." She grinned at her mother, and finally Moira found herself smiling back.

·   ·   ·

"It sounds like you've really thought this through," she said. "I'm happy for you."

"You don't like it, do you?" Candice said. "The house, I mean. I saw your face when you realized Eli and I had bought it."

Moira sighed. "It's not that I don't think it's a nice house. It really is; it's big, well built, and looks beautiful. It's just that I don't have very many good memories here. You know what happened to Zander, and then what happened with the previous owner."

"I know," Candice said. "That doesn't bother me, though. I don't believe in ghosts or any of that. I think that we'll make plenty of our own good memories here."

"You know what? I think you're right." She pulled her daughter into a tight hug. "Congratulations,

Candice. I'm so happy and excited for you and Eli. I really mean it."

CHAPTER FOURTEEN

Moira and Candice joined the others at the card table where they were filling their plates with snacks. David shot her a smile, which she returned. It looked like Eli had filled him in. She knew that this must be great news for him. He wouldn't have to worry any more about what would happen to the brewery. She had a feeling that he liked this place, despite all of the unfortunate things that had happened there. She would just have to try to do the same.

"So, Caroline, when do you go back home?" she asked, grabbing a paper plate and helping herself to some of the chips, salsa, and queso sauce.

. . .

"They're dropping me off at the airport after this," the dark-haired young woman said. "Hopefully I'll be able to come back soon. I love it out here. I'm so happy for Candice."

"Me too," Moira said. "This is a nice house. I'm glad that she and Eli like it so much."

It felt odd to think that this house would be her daughter's, hopefully for many years to come. It still felt like a stranger's house to her. She supposed that would change, given time. Once Candice moved her furniture in, along with her cat, Felix, it would probably start to feel more homey.

"What are you going to do with Reggie's house?" she asked Eli as she reached for a can of pop.

"We aren't sure yet," he admitted. "He's going to keep it for now. It's paid off, and he can easily afford the property taxes. It doesn't feel right to sell it, some-how. We may rent it out, preferably at a low price to someone we know. If Caroline ends up coming back like she's planning, she can stay there until she gets on her feet."

"It sounds like this is going to turn out perfectly for everyone," she said, smiling.

"Candice, Eli, are the two of you expecting anyone else?" David asked. He was looking out the window, a chip halfway to his mouth.

"What? No. Is someone here?" Candice hurried over. "Oh, my goodness. I don't believe it."

"What?" Eli asked.

"It's Alexa," she said. "Your crazy ex. Why won't she just leave us alone?"

· · ·

"Seriously? She's here?" He walked over to stand next to them.

Moira felt her stomach twist. Alexa, here, while the police were scouring the town for her. Had she come to finish off the job? Was she planning on hurting Candice?

"I'm going to go tell her this is unacceptable," Eli said. He pulled open the door and strode outside. Candice hesitated, then followed him. Caroline trailed along behind the two of them with a shrug, as if she was just along for the show.

"Candice, wait—" Moira sighed. "I'm going to go make sure no one gets hurt. David, will you call the police and tell them that their suspect is here?"

"All right. I'll be right behind you."

She hurried out the door and followed the three

younger people across the yard to where Alexa was busy attacking Eli's car.

"Lex, calm down," Eli said, approaching her. "What are you doing here?"

"I can't—" she yanked one of the back doors open with a grunt "—believe—" she hauled a suitcase out of the back seat "—you chose her—" the suitcase's contents went flying across the grass "—over me."

"That's my stuff!" Caroline yelped. Candice put a hand on her friend's arm.

"Let him deal with it. I don't think us getting closer would help."

"David's calling the police," Moira told her daughter. "She might be dangerous. Eli should get back."

.   .   .

"He knows what he's doing," Candice said.

At that moment, Alexa picked up something heavy from the spilled contents of the suitcase and hurled it at the car window, which shattered. Candice winced, and Caroline groaned.

"The statue I bought for my mom," she said. "What is *wrong* with this chick?"

Eli was approaching her slowly, taking one cautious step forward at a time. "Alexa, can you please stop breaking my car? Let's just sit down and talk about this."

"What is there to talk about?" Alexa snapped. "You made it perfectly clear that you'd rather be with *her* than with me."

"Yes, Candice is my fiancée," Eli said. "And that's not going to change. But attacking my car and destroying Caroline's stuff isn't going to help anything."

"You're right, *she's* the one who needs to go." Alexa threw something toward Candice, but it fluttered harmlessly to the ground just a few feet from her hand. A pair of socks.

"Hey, crazy," Caroline shouted. "You better get this outta your system before the police come, or you're going to be in even more trouble than you already are."

"You called the *police*?" Eli's ex wailed. "I just wanted to talk to him." She aimed another kick at his car. Eli reached for her, but she twisted away and, sobbing, started running down the driveway. He heaved a sigh.

"I really should go after her," he said reluctantly. "I think she's probably parked down around the curve. I wouldn't want her getting away."

. . .

"I'll come with you," Candice said.

"No, I don't want to risk her hurting you. If your mom's right, she might be the one who stole your car and killed Josh. That means she's dangerous."

Reluctantly, Candice stayed back while Eli jogged away. Moira put a hand on her shoulder. "I'm going to go see what's taking David so long," she said. "I think Eli's right, you should stay far away from Alexa."

"C'mon, Candice, let's go pet the cows or something. We'll hear the police when they pull up. Eli will be fine." Gently, Caroline guided her friend away. "Let the crazy girl be crazy somewhere else."

Moira shot one last glance at where Eli and Alexa had vanished around the curve of the driveway, then began the trudge back up to the house. David pushed through the screen door and met her halfway.

"The police are on their way," he said. "Sorry it took me a while. Jefferson had some information about the case." He paused and looked around. "Where is everyone?"

"Alexa ran off, Eli followed her so she wouldn't get away, and Caroline is trying to help Candice calm down, and also keep her away from Alexa," she told him. She realized how completely things had spiraled out of control.

"All right, I'll go after Alexa and Eli. Which way did they go?" She told him. "Thanks. Will you stay here in case the police show up before we get back?"

She reluctantly agreed, knowing that he was right, but not liking the idea of letting him and Eli do all of the dangerous work. It wouldn't feel right to just stand around and wait, but she couldn't see any

PATTI BENNING

other option. They needed the police to help with Alexa.

"Be careful, all right?" she said. "I love you."

"I love you, too." He paused long enough to kiss her, then turned to hurry away.

"David," she called out. He turned back to look at her. "What did Jefferson say about the case?"

"Nothing helpful," he said. "The hair that they got off of the back of Candice's seat was fake. It must have been from fake fur, on one of her coats or scarves or something."

He raised one hand in a quick wave goodbye, then jogged down the driveway after Eli and Alexa. Moira watched him until her rounded the curve, then sighed and went to go and wait by the cars. She hated feeling so useless.

. . .

She leaned against the hood of Eli's car, glancing occasionally toward the bend where her husband had vanished. *Maybe this place is cursed,* she thought. *What has my daughter gotten herself into?*

Too anxious to hold still, she began to pace. On her second circuit, something lying in the grass amongst the spilled contents of Caroline's suitcase caught her eye. It was a limp yellow thing. At first she thought it was some sort of dead animal. As she got closer, she realized what it was. A wig. A blonde wig. *The hair the police found was fake,* she thought. *Like faux fur... or a cheap wig.*

CHAPTER FIFTEEN

Could she possibly have been so wrong? She tried to remember every interaction she had had with Caroline since the girl had come back to Michigan. Had she missed something, some tiny clue that would have told her that the girl was out to get her daughter?

It doesn't make sense, she thought. *Why would someone that Candice considers one of her best friends try to frame her for murder?* She looked down at the messy wig. *Can there possibly be a good reason for Caroline to have a wig that matches my daughter's hair color so perfectly?* Try as she might, she couldn't think of one. Hoping that she was very mistaken, she began walking toward the dairy barn.

The barn was filled with cows. They were lined up on either side of the center aisle, and blinked at her calmly as she walked by. She saw Candice and Caroline down at the far end, and relief swept through her. Her daughter was fine, for the time being at least.

As she strode toward them, a cow behind her let out a low moo. The girls turned and saw her. Candice waved and began walking to meet her.

"Did Eli find Alexa?" she asked.

"Not yet. David went to help him," Moira said. "The police should be here soon."

"Good," her daughter said firmly. "I'm very ready for them to take her away."

.　.　.

"Candice," Caroline said. "It's getting late. I don't want to miss my flight."

"What time is it?" Candice glanced at her phone and frowned. "I'm sorry, Caroline, I didn't know all of this was going to happen. I don't know what to do. I guess I could borrow Eli's car and take you to the airport while everyone else deals with Alexa and the police, but that doesn't seem fair to them. Would you be okay with a later flight?"

"There isn't one, not until tomorrow."

"Well, I guess I can go see if I can find Eli's keys," Candice said dubiously.

"I don't think that's a good idea," Moira said. She didn't like the thought of Caroline getting one last chance alone with Candice. What if she decided to up the ante? If her new theory was right, then Caroline had already killed one person.

· · ·

"Why not?"

"Well, I'm sure the police will need to talk to you," she said.

"That's true. If Alexa really is the one that stole my car, then we're all going to need to talk to them." Candice sighed. "I'm sorry, Caroline, but this is just too important. A man is dead, and I can't miss my chance to help him get his justice. We'll just have to switch your flight to tomorrow."

Caroline reluctantly agreed. "Can we at least go and clean up my stuff before the police arrive?" she said. "I don't want a bunch of strange men looking at my undergarments."

"Sure." Candice gave a cow one last pat. "I do feel better, thanks for making me walk away and regroup. I'll help you clean up, then we can wait together for the guys to catch Alexa, or the police to get here, whichever happens first."

. . .

Relieved that the two women wouldn't be alone together, at least not until after the police arrived and could sort things out, Moira turned to go back the way she had come. She only made it a few steps before Caroline spoke up again.

"Hey, what's that?"

She turned to see the young woman staring at her. Moira brushed a hand against her back pocket and felt the blood rush out of her face. The wig. She thought she had stuffed it in deep enough, but a few hairs were hanging over the edge of the pocket. She met Caroline's gaze, and saw the younger woman's eyes first narrow, and then widen.

"What's what?" Candice asked, her voice light and curious. "Did you find something, Mom?"

. . .

"I…" The deli owner looked again at Caroline, trying to judge the girl's reaction. "Yes, I did, Candice." Deciding the truth was probably the best course of action, she pulled the rumpled wig out of her pocket and held it up in front of her with two fingers. "I found this in Caroline's luggage."

"I don't understand. What is it?" Candice peered at the thing. "Is that a wig?"

Her mother nodded.

"You had no right to go through my stuff," Caroline snapped. She stepped forward, reaching for it, but Moira took a matching step backward.

"I didn't go through anything," she reminded her. "It was lying on the grass. It fell out of your suitcase when Alexa was throwing stuff around."

"It's not mine," the other woman said.

. . .

"I thought you just said I had no right to go through your stuff? Isn't that implying that the wig is yours?"

Caroline glared daggers at her. "I must have packed it by accident. It must be from an old Halloween costume or something."

"Candice, there was one thing that never made sense about Alexa stealing your car," Moira said. "How would she have known how to hot-wire it? According to both the police and David, it wouldn't have been an easy feat. Somehow she doesn't strike me as the type to learn that sort of skill for fun."

"What are you saying, Mom?" Candice looked between her mother and her friend. "What's going on?"

"When you went to the convenience store the night

you came home from the bar, did you bring your keys with you?"

"I don't know," Candice said. "I guess not. I wasn't driving, and Eli had his keys. I don't think I even brought my purse."

"So, Caroline would have had access to your car key that night," Moira said flatly. The dark-haired young woman was pale, but Candice's face was beginning to flush as she put the pieces together. To the deli owner's surprise, her daughter's anger was directed not at her friend, but at her.

"Seriously, Mom? You've never liked Caroline. I knew you were going to do something like this. In fact, I'm surprised it took this long. You always thought she was a troublemaker. I'd hoped you'd have gotten over it by now."

"Candice, I'm not saying any of this because of how I felt about her when you were kids," her mother responded, hurt. "I actually felt terrible for trying to keep the two of you from being friends. I like her a lot now, or I thought I did before found this wig mixed in with her stuff."

"She wouldn't have any reason to steal my car," Candice said. "Besides, I trust her. She's my friend. I'm so sorry about this. I don't know what my mom's doing, but—" She turned to face her friend, then broke off mid-sentence. Moira realized that she had taken her eyes off of Caroline for just a second too long. The girl had found a pitchfork, and was pointing it at her friend.

"Stay back, both of you," she said. "Candice, where are Eli's keys?"

"What are you talking about?" Candice snapped. "Don't be ridiculous, Caroline. Put the pitchfork down. My mom's not going to turn you in. We both know you didn't do it, she's just holding a grudge from way back when we used to get in trouble together."

. . .

"You're so stupid," Caroline spat at her. "I'm not your *friend*. I only ever hung out with you back then because there was no one else around and you didn't care about getting in trouble. I didn't get why you kept trying to talk to me after I moved away. Half the time I never even answered you, but you just kept trying. How could you really think I cared?"

"Wha— Caroline, we were best friends." Candice stared at the other woman, hurt etched across her face. "If you didn't feel that way, why did you want to come out to visit?"

"You offered to pay for everything. Why would I turn a free trip down? I figured I'd keep in your good graces, have a good time, and maybe mooch a second trip out of you next year. It was actually kind of fun. I set up this whole persona for myself, and pretended to be the person you thought I was."

"I thought you wanted to move back here. You

wanted a job at the candy shop. We were going to let you live in Reggie's house while you figured stuff out."

"I was so insulted when you offered me a job. Like I want to spend my life working in a candy store for someone who's barely older than me. I mean, the free house was a good deal so I went along with it."

Moira edged toward her daughter as the two young women spoke, more concerned about getting between Candice and the dirty and sharp-looking pitchfork than what they were saying.

"So, is it true? You're the one that stole my car? Why would you do something like that?"

"Your life was so perfect. I wanted to mess things up for you. I thought if I drove around in your car, with that blonde wig—I picked it up at some second-hand shop in town one of the days you were working

—and did a bunch of stupid stuff, you might get in trouble with the law, or at least get a bad reputation."

"You *killed* someone," Candice said, aghast. "You *murdered* someone, just to make me look bad?"

For the first time, Caroline began to look uncomfortable. "I didn't mean to do that. When I took your car, I planned on just doing some dumb stuff, you know, smash a few mailboxes, do donuts in a parking lot where the security cameras would pick it up. I tossed a bunch of beer bottles in the back to make it look like you had been drinking, and was going to leave it behind the candy shop so the locals would see it in the morning. That guy, though, he just walked out of nowhere. I wasn't paying attention, and then he was right there, and I couldn't stop. I hit him, and I panicked, and I... I just kept going. I told myself he would be okay. I thought I'd just clipped him. I didn't know I killed him until I heard about it from you."

The pitchfork was shaking now. Careful not to make any sudden movements, Moira approached her slowly and pushed the tip down to the ground. Caroline tensed for a moment as she reached for the tool, then relaxed and let go of it. Still holding the weapon, the deli owner stepped toward one of the stalls. One of the cows sniffed her curiously.

"I seriously didn't mean to kill him. You believe me, right?" the young woman said, looking first at Candice, then at Moira. "I know I do stupid stuff sometimes, but I've never hurt someone that bad before."

"I know," Moira said, because it seemed like the right thing to say. "Come on, let's figure all of this out somewhere without twenty cows staring at us."

"Are you okay?" Moira asked her daughter. Candice was sitting on the wooden porch swing with her arms around her knees, gazing blankly toward the flashing lights of the police cars.

The past hour had been a chaotic mess. David and Eli had returned with Alexa just as the three women left the dairy barn. Caroline had tried to run away during the momentary distraction while they greeted each other, but with the private investigator, Eli, and Moira all on her tail, she hadn't managed to get far. After that, they had been at a loss at how to restrain the women, until Eli had had the bright idea to put them in his car. With Caroline in the front seat and Alexa in the back, and Eli, David, Moira, and Candice standing guard at each of the doors, it had proved an effective makeshift prison until the police arrived.

Then had come the whole mess of trying to explain to Detective Jefferson and the pair of officers that had tagged along what exactly had happened. Jefferson had questioned each of them individually, snapped a few pictures of the mess Alexa had made of the car, and had promised to contact Eli with instructions on how to go about getting a restraining order if he wanted one.

"I suggest getting one against her for both you and Candice," he had told the young man. "You have grounds and no shortage of witnesses; that way, if she comes near either of you again, she'll face some heavy charges. We're going to take her in right now for harassment, attempted assault, and destruction of property. Her family has enough money for a decent lawyer, so we probably won't be able to hold her for long. I'd get that restraining order as soon as possible."

. . .

Caroline, on the other hand, was looking at a much longer time behind bars. Moira was glad to know that the young woman would be seeing the justice she deserved for her crimes, but her sense of victory was tempered by the knowledge of how her daughter must be feeling just then.

"I don't really want to talk about it yet," Candice said. "It's just too much to really think about right now. But hey, you were right." She gave her mother a weak smile to show that she was joking.

"Well, I wish I had been wrong," Moira said. "I hope you know I'm here for you, if you need anything. I really am sorry, Candice."

"I know. You're a good person, Mom. I'm sorry I put you through so much when I was younger."

"We got through the tough times together, that's

what matters." She bent down to kiss the top of her daughter's head, then straightened up and looked toward the cars. One of the police vehicles was pulling away down the driveway, and the other followed soon after. David and Eli began the walk toward the house. She waved at her husband, and he waved back, giving her a tired smile that she recognized even from this distance. It had been a long and difficult day for all of them, but now it was over, and they were all together. As far as she was concerned, as long as her family was okay, things were all right.

ALSO BY PATTI BENNING

Papa Pacelli's Series

Book 1: Pall Bearers and Pepperoni

Book 2: Bacon Cheddar Murder

Book 3: Very Veggie Murder

Book 4: Italian Wedding Murder

Book 5: Smoked Gouda Murder

Book 6: Gourmet Holiday Murder

Book 7: Four Cheese Murder

Book 8: Hand Tossed Murder

Book 9: Exotic Pizza Murder

Book 10: Fiesta Pizza Murder

Book 11: Garlic Artichoke Murder

Book 12: On the Wings of Murder

Book 13: Mozzarella and Murder

Book 14: A Thin Crust of Murder

Book 33: A Melted Morsel of Murder

Book34: A Saucy Taste of Murder

Book 35: A Crunchy Crust of Murder

Book 36: Shrimply Sublime Murder

Book 37: Boldly Basil Murder

Darling Deli Series

Book 1: Pastrami Murder

Book 2: Corned Beef Murder

Book 3: Cold Cut Murder

Book 4: Grilled Cheese Murder

Book 5: Chicken Pesto Murder

Book 6: Thai Coconut Murder

Book 7: Tomato Basil Murder

Book 8: Salami Murder

Book 9: Hearty Homestyle Murder

Book 10: Honey BBQ Murder

Book 11: Beef Brisket Murder

Book 12: Garden Vegetable Murder

Book 31: Shamrocks and Murder

Book 32: Sugar Coated Murder

Book 33: Murder, My Darling

Killer Cookie Series

Book 1: Killer Caramel Cookies

Book 2: Killer Halloween Cookies

Book 3: Killer Maple Cookies

Book 4: Crunchy Christmas Murder

Book 5: Killer Valentine Cookies

Asheville Meadows Series

Book 1: Small Town Murder

Book 2: Murder on Aisle Three

Book 3: The Heart of Murder

Book 4: Dating is Murder

Book 5: Dying to Cook

Book 6: Food, Family and Murder

Book 7: Fish, Chips and Murder

Cozy Mystery Tails of Alaska

Book 1: Mushing is Murder

Book 2: Murder Befalls Us

Book 3: Stage Fright and Murder

Book 4: Routine Murder

Book 5: Best Friends and Betrayal

Book 6: Tick Tock and Treachery

AUTHOR'S NOTE

I'd love to hear your thoughts on my books, the storylines, and anything else that you'd like to comment on—reader feedback is very important to me. My contact information, along with some other helpful links, is listed on the next page. If you'd like to be on my list of "folks to contact" with updates, release and sales notifications, etc.... just shoot me an email and let me know. Thanks for reading!

Also...

... if you're looking for more great reads, Summer Prescott Books publishes several popular series by outstanding Cozy Mystery authors.

CONTACT SUMMER PRESCOTT BOOKS PUBLISHING

Twitter: @summerprescott1

Bookbub: https://www.bookbub.com/authors/ summer-prescott

Blog and Book Catalog: http://summerprescottbooks.com

Email: summer.prescott.cozies@gmail.com

YouTube: https://www.youtube.com/channel/ UCngKNUkDdWuQ5k7-Vkfrp6A

And...be sure to check out the Summer Prescott Cozy Mysteries fan page and Summer Prescott

Books Publishing Page on Facebook – let's be friends!

To download a free book, and sign up for our fun and exciting newsletter, which will give you opportunities to win prizes and swag, enter contests, and be the first to know about New Releases, click here: http://summerprescottbooks.com

Made in the USA
Las Vegas, NV
11 September 2024

95135307R00095